SHINE-A-LIGHT
PRESS

For permissions, please email Shine-A-Light Press at info@ShineALightCorp.com.
Shine-A-Light Press and related logo are registered trademarks of Shine-A-Light, Corp.

Copyright ©2021, Alysha Brooke Abrams
Book edit, layout and design by Chris and Andrea Elston

Educators and librarians, for a variety of teaching tools to use with this book,
visit us at www.shinealightpress.com

First paperback edition published by Shine-A-Light Press and printed in October 2021

Summary:
Born from an actual conversation between the author and her son, this amazingly illustrated picture book paints a beautiful picture of diversity by exploring the abundance of color in God's creation; showing that differences in our skin color was part of His perfect plan from the beginning of time.

Library of Congress Control Number: 2021947845

ISBN 978-1-953158-90-1
50899

9 781953 158901

Printed in the U.S.A.
U.S.A. $8.99

The
Color of GOD

Written by Alysha Brooke Abrams

Illustrated by Katherine Schmid

Dedicated to my Micah David. The most contagiously joyful human being I have ever met. You are by far my greatest accomplishment in life. I never truly knew God until the day you were born. You will forever be mommy's little angel.

Thank you to my parents, Robert and Cindy, for always pushing me to pursue my dreams. And to my grandma, Ann, for always believing in me, even when I didn't believe in myself.

~

"I praise you, for I am fearfully and wonderfully made.
Wonderful are your works, my soul knows it very well."
Psalm 139:14

Author's Note

Being part of a multi-racial family, my sweet boy never thought much about skin color since so many shades are represented all around him. It wasn't until the Summer of 2020, when racial injustice became so prevalent once again, that sweet Micah David started to have some questions. As we drove by a busy intersection, the street corners were covered with signs that said, "BLACK LIVES MATTER". Micah said to me, *"Mommy, why are people holding those signs? Why do they need to say that? Why wouldn't black lives matter?"* That was the first time I ever had to speak to my child about racism. Our social circle shrunk as opposing sides debated the realness of systemic racism, social unrest, and the call for justice. I cried with my cousin and friends over the fear we carry in raising children, especially boys, in a world where this still exists. As I raised prayers to my Creator and asked Jesus to protect my little boy and his innocence, the most natural and organic conversation occurred between me and my Micah David, and this book is simply an embellishment of what that conversation looked like. This story is God-breathed, with a timely message that the next generation needs desperately to hear – we are *all* created equally, wonderfully made, and an absolute reflection of the perfect God who designed us. "No matter the color, no matter the shade, EVERY. SINGLE. LIFE. GOD. HAS. MADE."

With Hope for A Better Future,

Alysha

P.S. Some helpful words to know in this story:

Saba – Hebrew for Grandfather
Dobie – Hebrew for Teddy Bear
Tia – Spanish for Auntie
Kahue – is a Hawaiian name and Micah's Godfather

One glorious, sunny, summer day
As Micah David was going out to play
He asked his Mommy,

"Have you ever noticed
or seen?
Your skin is different
than the skin
GOD gave me?"

"Yes!" Mommy smiled and said,
as she laid her hand on the back of his head,

"Different is just what GOD likes to do . . .
and guess what?

I absolutely LOVE that about you!"

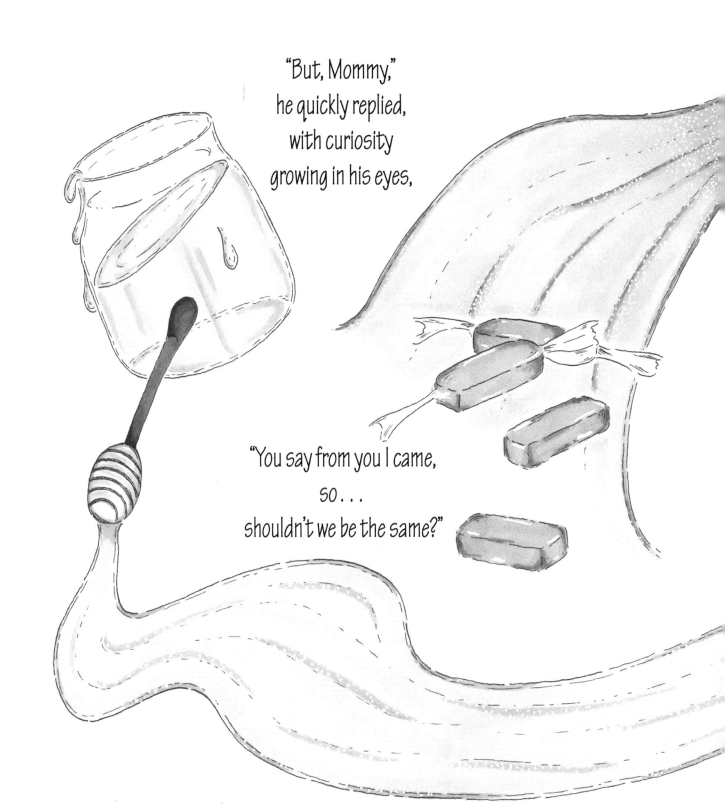

"But, Mommy,"
he quickly replied,
with curiosity
growing in his eyes,

"You say from you I came,
so . . .
shouldn't we be the same?"

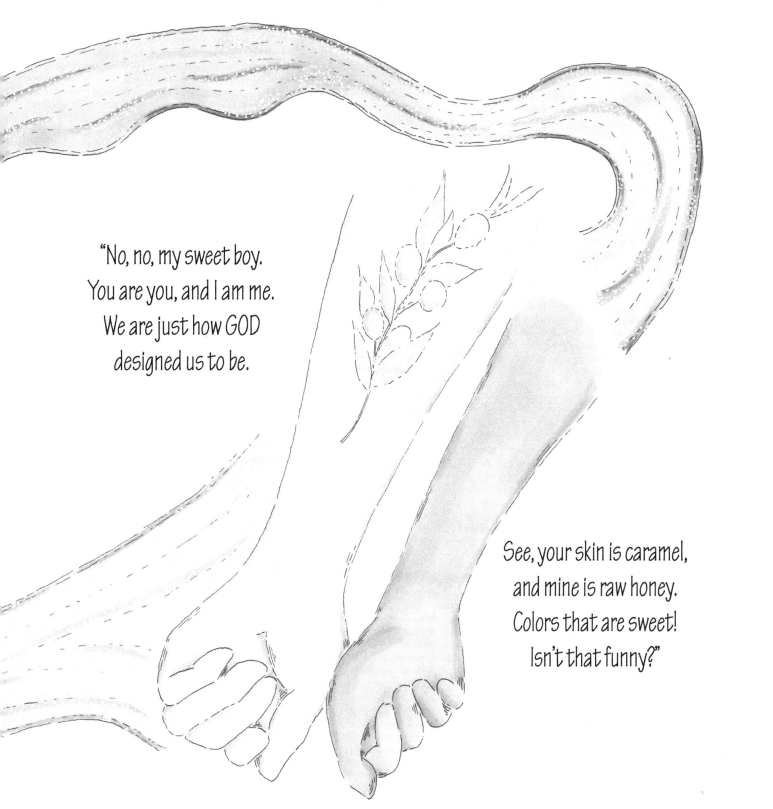

"No, no, my sweet boy.
You are you, and I am me.
We are just how GOD
designed us to be.

See, your skin is caramel,
and mine is raw honey.
Colors that are sweet!
Isn't that funny?"

"But, Mommy. I don't understand.
Why is making us different part of GOD's plan?"

Taking his hand, Mommy walked him outside.
She looked around, took a breath,
and sent a prayer to the skies.

"Look at the mountains,
the flowers and the trees.

Look all around
and tell me,
what do you see?"

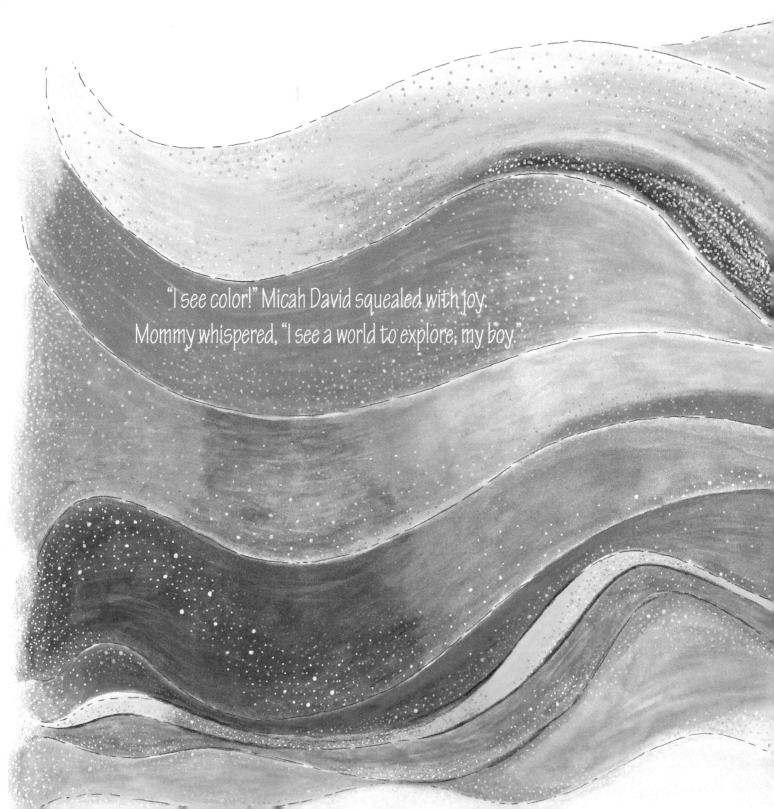

"I see color!" Micah David squealed with joy.
Mommy whispered, "I see a world to explore, my boy."

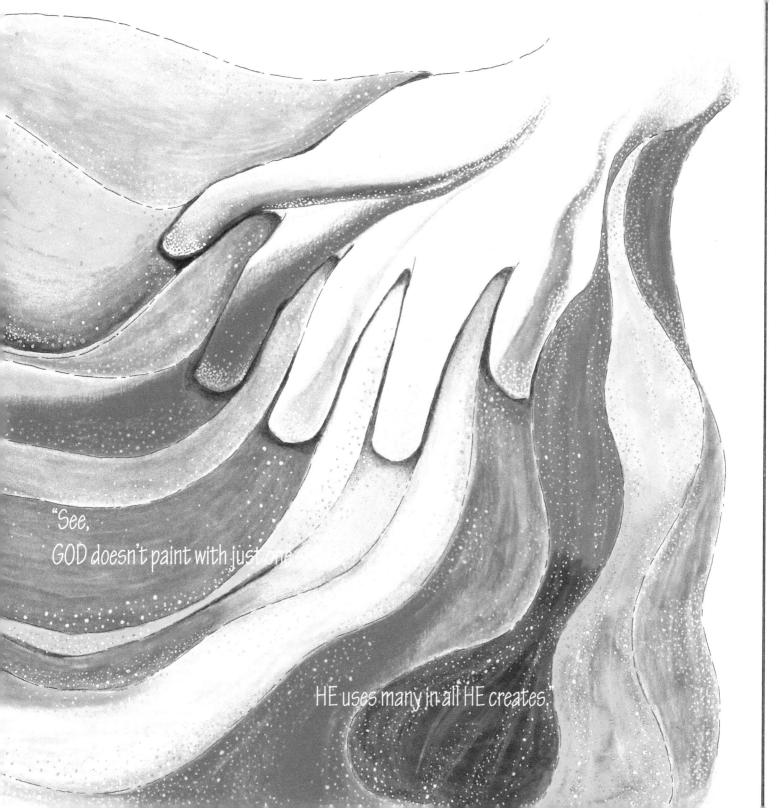

"See,
GOD doesn't paint with just one.

HE uses many in all HE creates."

"In the sky, HE paints
with different shades of blue;

teal, aquamarine and indigo, too."

"Sometimes, HE even adds a touch of periwinkle or slate —
depending the weather, depending the day."

"And look at the flowers, dancing in the wind!

Tulips aren't just red.
They are cherry, garnet,
and scarlet instead."

"And the daffodils! They aren't simply yellow, are they?

They are the color of
pineapple, Tuscan sun,
and canary!"

"Look over there!
Tell me what you see!"
Micah David shouted,
"I see lots of really green trees!"

"Yes, my baby,
but those aren't just green!
They are emerald, pistachio,
moss, and seaweed!

Juniper, basil, fern, and lime!
Just like GOD's people, different by design!"

"Colors aren't just colors.
There are
SO MANY shades!
And by a loving GOD,
all of them
are made!"

"Our family represents
many pieces of the world.
We are colorful,
and different in our herd."

"Look at Saba.
What color is he?"
"He is like me!
We can call him a caramel toffee."

"I love it," said Mommy, "now who is next?"

"How about Mimi?
She can be a sugar cookie mix!"

Mommy said laughing, "Yes! Let's keep going . . .
what other yummy shades is our family showing?"

"Daniel is buttermilk, and Kahue is beige.
Auntie Desi is sand and Uncle Monzelle is clay!"

"Nanny is cantaloupe and Auntie Dobie is peach!
Uncle Brent is ginger and Ms. Kelli is taffy."

"Andria is vanilla, Steph is cream.
Uncle Pat is as light as a Saltine!"

"Alex is cider and Auntie D is bronze.
Gabby is blush and baby Ross is fawn.
Tia Lily, granola and Teresa, Dijon!"

"It always amazes me,
how many colors GOD creates!
Like macaroon, oat, biscotti, and date!"

"Mommy," Micah David said with a little frown slipping in.

"All these shades explain the color of you and me, but what color is GOD? What color is HE?"

Mommy crouched down
taking Micah David's
face in her hand,
as she whispered,
"HE's all of them.
Every color in this land."

"Every human life is created in the image of GOD
no matter the complexion, HE represents them all!"

"No matter the color, no matter the shade,
EVERY. SINGLE. LIFE. GOD. HAS. MADE."

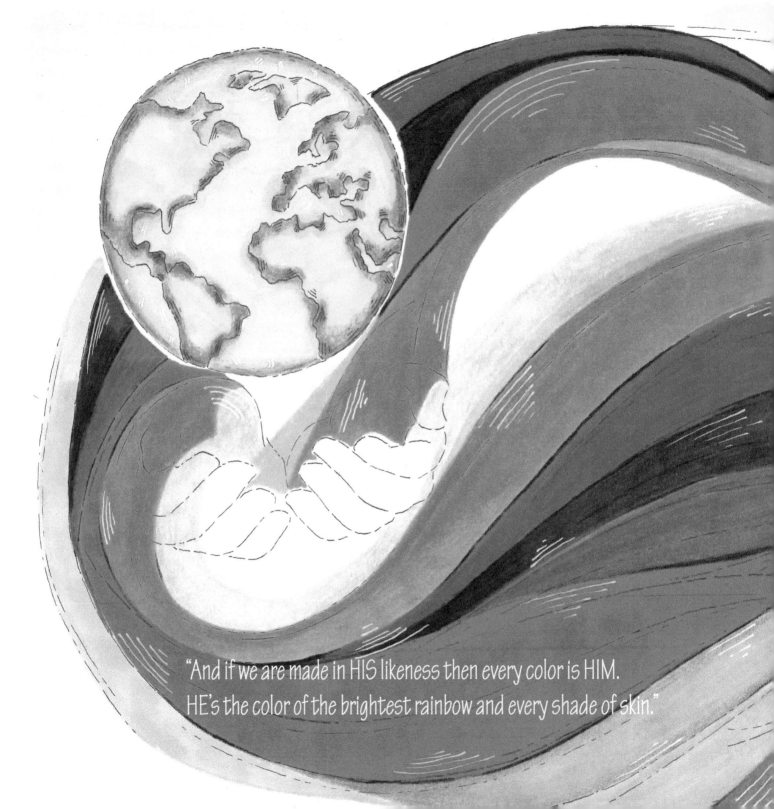

"And if we are made in HIS likeness then every color is HIM.
HE's the color of the brightest rainbow and every shade of skin."

"The color of GOD really can't be explained.
HE's simply the color of everything HE's ever made."

"I understand now, Mommy!" Micah David exclaimed,
and his frown reversed to a smile again.

"GOD is the same color as me AND YOU!"

"Exactly!" Mommy said,
overjoyed he knew
TRUTH.

And away they walked,
toward the sun,

through golden sunflowers clothed
in chartreuse and cinnamon.

ABOUT THE AUTHOR

My name is Alysha Brooke Abrams and I am the proud single-mama to one beautiful, energetic little boy! I have spent my entire life in the Pacific Northwest - the trees and the water are where I feel most at home and most connected to God. I am a huge book nerd and LOVE to read, I've also had a deep desire to paint with words for as long as I can remember.

I am in administration at a private school in the greater Seattle area and feel blessed to be part of the educational system, helping shape the hearts and minds of the next generation. I love to cook, garden, hike, forest bathe and explore the outdoors in my down time. I'm also very involved in my church and love to serve others.

ABOUT THE ILLUSTRATOR

My name is Katie Schmid and my love for art has always been part of me from a young age. I attended Northwest College of Art in Washington State, graduating with a BA in graphic design and fine art. My favorite mediums to use are pen and ink and acrylic paints.

I'm married to a loving husband, Chris, and am the proud mom to three boys: Noah, Jonah, and Micah. Being part of this beautiful children's book with Alysha has been an amazing blessing.

CPSIA information can be obtained
at www.ICGtesting.com
Printed in the USA
LVHW071353011121
702131LV00021B/978